W9-ATS-920

Silver Press

Library of Congress Cataloging-in-Publication Data

Kraus, Robert, 1925-
Buggy Bear cleans up / by Robert Kraus.
p. cm.
Summary: Buggy Bear, who never takes a bath or washes his clothes, alienates the other animals in Miss Gator's school, until he falls in love with a classmate and decides to change his ways.
[1. Cleanliness—Fiction. 2. Bears—Fiction. 3. Schools—Fiction. 4. Animals—Fiction.]
I. Title. II. Series: Kraus, Robert, 1925– Miss Gator's schoolhouse.
PZ7.K868Bt 1989
[E]—dc20 89-10221
CIP
ISBN 0-671-68608-9 AC
ISBN 0-671-68612-7 (pbk.)

Produced by Parachute Press, Inc.

Published by Silver Press, a division of
Silver Burdett Press, Inc.
Simon & Schuster, Inc.,
Prentice Hall Bldg., Englewood Cliffs, NJ 07632.
Printed in the United States of America.
10 9 8 7 6 5 4 3 2 1

Chapter 1
ALL ABOUT BUGGY

Buggy Bear wasn't neat.

In fact, Buggy was very sloppy.

Buggy Bear slept in his clothes.

He woke up every morning
and didn't even wash his face.

He also didn't brush his teeth.

He didn’t take a bath either.

How could he?

He didn’t have a bathtub.

“Why should I take a bath?”

said Buggy.

“I took one in the swamp

last year.”

Buggy just gobbled, slurped,

and sloshed his breakfast.

Then he set off for the
little red schoolhouse
in the swamp.
One morning on his way
to school...

Buggy fell into a mud puddle.

It wasn't the first time.

"If there's a mud puddle around,

Buggy Bear will fall into it,"

hissed Blake the Snake.

“Buggy likes mud,” said Ella
the Bad Speller. “M-U-D-D.”
“Stop picking on Buggy,”
said Punky Skunky.
“Who’s picking? Who’s picking?”
said Tardy Toad—late as usual.

As soon as they got to school
it was time for fingernail inspection.

Everyone lined up—
except Blake the Snake.
He had no fingernails.

OPQRSTU V

Everyone passed the fingernail test—except Buggy Bear.
"Oh, dear," said Miss Gator. "You could plant a vegetable garden in all that dirt."
"Not a bad idea," said Buggy.
"I love vegetables."

OPQRSTUVWXYZ

“What a pig that bear is,”

said Ella the Bad Speller.

“That’s an insult to pigs,”

hissed Blake the Snake.

"Buggy's buggy," said Tardy Toad.

"And Tardy's tardy."

"I think Buggy's kind of cute,"

said Punky Skunky.

"If only he would clean up his act."

“Buggy Bear,” said Miss Gator.
“I’d like to have a little talk
with you.”
Miss Gator took Buggy outside
where there was lots
of fresh air.

"Buggy Bear," said Miss Gator.

"You've got to clean up.

You're a disgrace to bears.

You're a dirty bear."

"But I like being dirty,"

said Buggy.

"But you smell," said Miss Gator.

"Me, smell?"

"Yes, you smell!" hissed Blake.

"What can I do?" asked Buggy.

"Wash," said Miss Gator.

"That's what we all do."

"I'd rather stay buggy,"
said Buggy.
But nobody heard him.

As you can imagine,
Buggy's friends all kept
their distance.

THEN A FUNNY THING HAPPENED.

Chapter 2
BUGGY LOVES PUNKY

Buggy Bear fell in love
with Punky Skunky.

He fell like a ton of bricks.

All he could think of was Punky.

Punky. Punky. Punky.

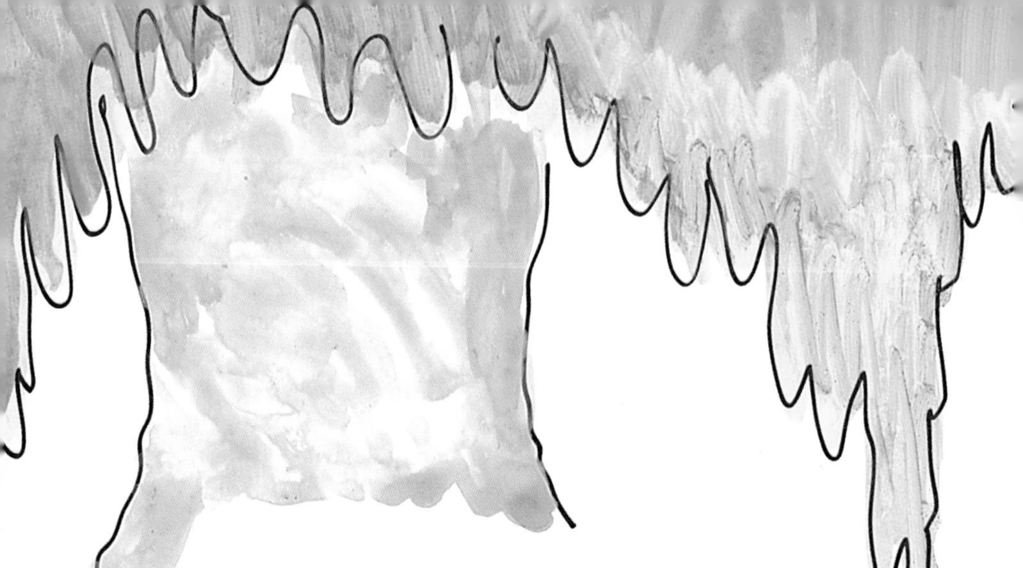

But Buggy was too shy
to tell Punky.
He told Blake the Snake instead.
“I love Punky,” said Buggy.
“But she won’t come near me.”
“Who can blame her?”
hissed Blake the Snake.

“What should I do?” asked Buggy.

“Just come with me,” said Blake.

Blake took Buggy to his house
to take a bath.

But Blake’s snake bathtub
was not the right shape for Buggy.

?
KEEP CLEAN
BLAKE'S BATH

"Where there's a will,

there's a way," said Blake.

He filled a washtub with water.

"Jump in, Buggy," said Blake.

Buggy jumped in.

"It's wet!" said Buggy.

“This is the way

we scrub our clothes,

scrub our clothes,

scrub our clothes,” sang Blake.

“And hang them
out to dry!”

Then Blake taught Buggy how to wash his face and behind his ears.

He taught him how to brush his teeth...

and how to comb his hair.

"Now look in the mirror,"

said Blake.

"I look nice," said Buggy.

"You smell nice, too,"

said Blake.

"Thanks, Blake," said Buggy.

"You're a true friend."

Chapter 3
THE NEW BUGGY

The next day on the way to school, Buggy picked some swamp flowers to give to Punky Skunky.

“I picked these for you, Punky,”

said Buggy.

“Thanks, Buggy,” said Punky.

"Oh, gosh," said Buggy, blushing.

All the kids in Miss Gator's class smiled when Buggy sat down at his desk.

Especially Punky Skunky.

At recess, Tardy Toad said,
"Now that you don't smell,
Buggy, I might even
come to school on time."
"You're so clean,"
said Ella the Bad Speller.
"K-L-E-E-N."

Everybody looked at Buggy.

But Buggy had eyes only for Punky.

At last, Buggy said it.

"I love you, Punky."

"I love you, too, Buggy,"

said Punky.

“Oh, gosh,” said Buggy,

and he fell smack dab into

the biggest mud puddle ever.

And Buggy Bear was

buggy again!